Jim Williams is a young man from Greece who has a thirst for knowledge. He's studying hard for academic achievements, and he's writing more and more stories to enrich his mythologies.

With a vibrant imagination and a flair for the dramatic, all seems possible to him.

His never-ending quest continues.

To my dearest mother, who still inspires me with her actions and selfless choices about life!

Jim Williams

THE TALES OF HIDDEN TRUTH II

The Other Side

AUSTIN MACAULEY PUBLISHERS™
LONDON · CAMBRIDGE · NEW YORK · SHARJAH

Copyright © Jim Williams 2024

The right of Jim Williams to be identified as author of this work has been asserted by the author in accordance with sections 77 and 78 of the Copyright, Designs and Patents Act 1988.

All rights reserved. No part of this publication may be reproduced, stored in a retrieval system, or transmitted in any form or by any means, electronic, mechanical, photocopying, recording, or otherwise, without the prior permission of the publishers.

Any person who commits any unauthorised act in relation to this publication may be liable to criminal prosecution and civil claims for damages.

This is a work of fiction. Names, characters, businesses, places, events, locales, and incidents are either the products of the author's imagination or used in a fictitious manner. Any resemblance to actual persons, living or dead, or actual events is purely coincidental.

A CIP catalogue record for this title is available from the British Library.

ISBN 9781035845880 (Paperback)
ISBN 9781035845897 (ePub e-book)

www.austinmacauley.com

First Published 2024
Austin Macauley Publishers Ltd®
1 Canada Square
Canary Wharf
London
E14 5AA

Table of Contents

Part One   9

Act I: The Graceful Assassin   14

Act II: Destined Doom   17

Act III: Dance of the Butterflies   20

Act IV: Prelude of the Finale   22

Act V: A moonlit Finale   25

Part Two   29

Chapter One: The Warrior with the Butterfly Tattoo   31

Chapter Two: A Merry Golden- Haired Girl, Azure   33

Chapter Three: Azure's Task, a New Journey Begins   37

Chapter Four: Heading Westward, the Witch of the Shadows Attacks   44

Chapter Five: The Master Blacksmith, Alexandrea the Wildfire   48

Chapter Six: The Legendary Moon Sword   53

Chapter Seven: The Shadow Returns, a New Star is Added to the Sky   56

Chapter One: Vs the Illusionist Faceless Mage   62

Chapter Two: Black Alchemy   64

Chapter Three: Vs the Witch of the Greenfields   68

Chapter Four: Visit to the Witch of the Black Forest   71

Chapter Five: Tackling the Past   74

Chapter Six: The Journey into the Land of Mystics   78

Chapter Seven: Weaving the Threads of Destiny   82

Chapter Eight: The Fall of the Mystics   85

Chapter Nine: A Touch of Destiny   87

Chapter Ten: Looking Back, and Moving Forward   91

Part One

It was absurd, everybody knew. Only men were allowed to battle. It wasn't anybody's fault for that, but it was a problem nonetheless; for she wanted to battle, she wanted to honour her family, but most importantly her late father, whom she loved dearly.

She lived in a wee little village, far away from the citadel, where the five ruled. The village's neighbour was Bowerea, the city of the fabled Grand Priest, so it was only natural to be influenced by his teachings. The Grand Priest strongly believed that only men should join conquests. It was a man's job to die in the fray. It was a man's job to lead, fight, and die.

The woman's role was vital still, though. She had to stay behind at home and take care of the children. She was to educate them and see to it that they would be either mighty warriors or good wives. For the Priest, the woman's role in society was the most important one. It was her and her feelings of affection that would determine whether the children would succeed in fulfilling their role in life or not.

That was what the Grand Priest believed, and everyone who followed him came to believe it too; and even if they didn't believe it, they'd still exercise the same practices anyway. Although he didn't have a kingdom under his command, surprisingly enough, all the neighbouring villages chose to follow his teachings.

The women there were actually happy and proud they had such an important role within the family, but as expected there were some few exceptions that desired more than that. There were some that tried to dress like men and enrol into the army, but they were discovered and they were immediately executed. A couple of others chose to make their difference by going to the camp, before their march, to bid farewell to the warriors. This gesture was reluctantly accepted, and it was due to the fact that two warriors vowed to marry them if they ever got back. And lastly, the one that desired more is the one this part of the tale revolves around. She chose to wear a traditional costume of men and a mask, and with that disguise, she went to challenge the Priest himself.

She slithered through the guards all the way to the Priest's chambers, where he seemingly awaited her arrival. She then demanded an audience and claimed that it was for supremacy. He, feeling that she bluffed, accepted her challenge. She had chosen the alias 'James' for that battle, which little did she know as to how ambiguous that was…

The battle started. She unleashed a barrage of swift swings with her long sword, but the Priest saw them all coming, and he smoothly dodged each and every one of them. He then countered with a stream of fire; but she intercepted by swinging her sword hard, cutting the stream in half and immediately issuing a counterattack.

He then raised his hand and stopped the fight. He said: "Well done, O Lady of the Forest, you may not be a man, but you definitely have the skill to join a battle and win. However, that is precisely why you must stay behind and make sure the next generation will take a step into the future, the right one!"

She was mesmerised. He must've known all along, and what's more, he just acknowledged her skills. But she wanted more…

"I can see two pathways laid ahead of you, but first, I must ask you never to use the name 'James' again, for he is a person that will stretch all the way to the future, someone who will hold destiny in his hands with another!" said the Priest and sighed. "Alas, time is growing shorter by the second, so allow me to continue. One course is with you returning home to educate the young, and the other, the one that it's more likely for you to choose, is the one where you join the battle in the Yonderland, north of here, and meet glory and anguish. But be warned: the pathway to glory goes hand in hand with heartache and despair!"

She was in awe, but she had already decided the course she'd follow. The battlefield called out to her, and as far as she was concerned, she had no heart to ache. She smiled.

"I see that you made up your mind, so let me give you a few last words before you leave my palace!" the Priest said and sat comfortably on his throne. "For starters, while you travel and while you fight you should always keep your outfit and mask on; that way, you will begin to comprehend the life you've been envying and what kind of person you were hoping to be. Secondly, you must be careful of the bright blue butterfly, for it might prove to be fatal for you. And lastly, I will give you something different, something that when I first came to understand it, I began living anew… 'One must know oneself under the rain, or under the sun, or under the moon. By accepting oneself one can live, by knowing thyself one can walk freely; but be warned, if one were to lose oneself into meaningless wonder of identity, one is sure to crumble, one is sure to walk into peril!'"

With that, he slightly bowed his head and she did the same, while being completely mesmerised and deeply honoured, because the Grand Priest himself took his time to speak to her, he took his time to compliment her and to warn her.

She then took her leave, but as she left the palace an uncomfortable feeling sat on her chest. She felt that this was the last time she'd meet the Grand Priest; and little did she know that that feeling would turn out to be true...

She immediately made her preparations to travel to the Yonderland Valley; to join the fray that would come to be known in the future as a mythical conquest where multiple legends came to be. She didn't return to her village, the last time she laid her eyes on it was when she sneaked out of it, never sharing a farewell word with anyone.

She went to Mount Gold to prepare body and soul. During her stay there, she managed to truly ascend to a higher level of power. She harmonised completely with Mother Nature and surprisingly enough she managed to do so thanks to the very special locals that resided there. They were colourful butterflies, very special indeed.

Mainly she accomplished such a great feat by meditating and consciously waving her sword within her psychic world. The butterflies seemed eager to help her, which she interpreted as a sign for the Priest's divination. She, of course, thought that that was the end of it in the end, that the butterflies were simply curious; and who can blame her? She truly believed she could escape her destiny...

While still being there, she decided to knit another costume. She did it by taking the silk from the crawly creatures of the forest. She crafted a new mask, as well, with wood taken from an old willow tree. The costume was beautiful, plain red and white whilst flowers were woven on the sleeves, while the mask was horrid, with three horns on top and dead leaves on the edges.

She was ready. She marched towards the battle. She wouldn't take any side, she would be no one's ally, but everyone would be her enemy; and because of that notion, she didn't bother learning the names of the armies and the cities they represented. She only wanted to slash...she was not yet aware of...

As she closed in on the valley, she had to cross a ravine to reach the battle's core. At that ravine, another battle raged on between two other cities, each of which supported one of the main opposing forces.

Act I: The Graceful Assassin

"Sakura blossoms dance,
Wind howled, resounding echoes,
Throughout it reaches,
It masks, it loves it all,

Splattered spots everywhere,
Red and black whirl around,
Vividly it springs,
Like waterfall it sprays,

The count is high,
Indifferent for identity she was,
All were equal,
Her silver blade danced around."

A scene of disaster was, after she was done with them. Both sides were obliterated, she didn't lose a single step. It was like a dramatic play, like those plays that were held in a country of light in a distant and parallel universe, where tragedies took shape. Only in this play, things were completely one-sided.

She bathed in red, and she loved every second of it. She felt alive as her sword sang. The sky was painted blue, the rocks were dyed red. She danced smoothly as she was walking on clouds. She looked so peaceful, and yet she still didn't notice…

As she walked, she came to realise that she occasionally would have to jump from rock to rock if she wanted to reach her destination, for the road abruptly ended from time to time. That was a bit of a challenge for her, for she had never trained her balance for that kind of exercise, and most importantly she was quite overdressed.

As expected of her, though, she managed to do it. She theatrically jumped from one point to the next, while slashing everything and anything in her path that was alive. She was a changed person.

"The sun is now falling,
Orange deep it cloaks it all,
The sorrow runs deep,
As she had lost her way,

The sunrays bleed,
Glory is gained,
The prize will be steep,
When she'll be force to pay it,

The time grows near,
Nothing's free,
Some pay with blood,
Some pay with tears."

She climbed down, and night fell along with her. As the starry sky showed his face, she looked pale; but behind that pale exterior, a massive fiery passion was hidden well.

Act II: Destined Doom

"The night was dame,
She danced for knight,
Chorus: {O great night}
To find the stallion,
{O great night}
Who will make her cry,
Bittersweet will forever be,
But she loved to tangle,
{She loved it all}
She craved to mingle,
{She loved it all}
All her whims were shifting,
Towards her, crippled went,
Emotions were scarce and tired,
{She never had}
She's vengeful always,
{She'll always be}
She never halted, always forward,
Grandeur of dreams,
{Dreams of grandeur}
She'll always fail,
{She'll always fail}."

She was about to reach the ravine's core, and into the main battle, until a certain someone stood in her way; a couple of warriors did so, while not intentionally. They were wrapped in a battle to the death.

She simply observed their battle. It may have been a serious duel, with everything at stake, but it was a stunning performance nonetheless, she was genuinely touched by their resolve.

Butterflies danced around them. She became enraged, thinking that this scene was destined to take place in front of her, which is why all of it was doomed to end in the dramatic way it did…

"Assault, attack, atrocity,
Chorus: {Oh, Ah, Oh, Ah}
Nothing compares,
{Nothing compares}
All is lost for them,
{All is lost}
All for naught it was,
{All for naught}
Injustice struck,
{Injustice struck}
They could only see,
{They could only}
The shadow of dusk,
{The shadow of}
Then all was lost,
{All was lost}
The butterflies saw,
{The butterflies saw}

She made it finally,
{Finally she did}
Fatal the mistake,
{Fatal mistake}
Gloating can be indeed,
{Indeed can it be}
A sin of deadly spin,
{Deadly spin}
The butterflies leered in,
{Butterflies leered}."

After the onslaught ended, she adjusted her mask and moved forward. Completely indifferent to the massacre she left behind. The butterflies hovered.

Act III: Dance of the Butterflies

There was no end to it; she craved more…more blood, more slashing, more suffering, more of it all. She had just left behind her a scene filled with carnage, but it wasn't nearly enough; she wanted more.

She walked down the line, deeper into the ravine. She walked slowly, elegantly, but her desire burned her heart. There was no doubt in her mind; she was getting close; she could smell the enemy's fear. Her invigoration and high expectations went up in smoke after a certain 'dance' took place before her eyes.

"A dreaded dance it was,
Chorus: {As they glided}
They hummed a tune with it,
{As they glowed}
Beautiful it was, and yet,
{The ruthless warrior was caught}
It was a hum of impending doom,
Synchronised, dashing, colourful,
Pale blue it was for long,
{Terror was born}
They never missed a step,
{Terror ensnared}

How could they, indeed?
{Moments stood still}
They were hatched from cocoons of old,
{Nothing endured}
Melodies wore them brightly,
Tunes that she produced,
{It was done}
The one who held the moonlight,
{It was over}
The one who walked eternal dawn,
{The warrior was judged}
Her destiny was now sealed, forevermore,
{The moonlight now bathed her}."

Act IV: Prelude of the Finale

Infuriated she was. Those filthy butterflies were ruining her perfect view; dancing and glowing, how dare they? They were lucky she was in a forgiving mood at the time, and she let them go; but in her fury, she started slashing everything and anything around her. Flowers and trees were gone; they were mercilessly cut down.

"Was it dusk?
Chorus: {What was it?}
Was it dawn?
{What was it?}
Difficult to tell, indeed,
{What was it?}
As she walked down the line,
{She walked}
She was about to meet him,
{She'll meet}
Her archenemy, the bitter one,
{He was there}
The duel that was foretold,
{Upcoming battle}
The duel that was meant to be,

{Fated battle}
She didn't know, however,
{Ignorant she was}
They were present,
{They were close}
They were safe and watched,
{They were hidden}
As she walked towards him,
{Ignorant she was}
There he was, patient,
{His latent powers}
Wait, he did, confident and true,
{He's unsurpassed}."

She laid her eyes on him. She hated him right away, but there was something else too…this time, she felt something else…for the first time, she felt fear, although she'd never admit it. But regardless of her inner conflict, she had a clear idea of what she had to do; she had to eliminate him, permanently.

"It was like a dance,
A dreadful fight for survival,
A massive fight of will,
Brilliant slashes,
His red hair taken in by wind,
Her mask hid her fear,
His broad smile shone,
Her sword became dull,
His red blade glowed,
Her hopes faded away,

Relentless and fearless he was,
Wrapped in fear she was,
For she knew it in her heart,
Her time had finally come."

    She was on her knees, for she had lost the duel. He stood in front of her, the victor. He didn't say anything. He simply scoffed and walked away; she was angered.

    "What are you doing, you miserable man? Finish me off!" said she, trying to catch her breath. He then stopped but didn't turn. He scoffed again.

    "You don't deserve that… I can't force my moon-sword to slay vermin like you!" said he, completely disgusted by her.

    "Why you…!" she gave a shriek as she was laying on the ground, looking helpless as he walked away…but as he was going in the distance, she saw it…she saw the butterfly tattoo on his neck…she saw the butterfly.

Act V: A moonlit Finale

Bathed in shame, she lay on the ground floor, unable to move, helpless as a newborn bird.

"Bitter it was indeed,
Chorus: {Bitter it was}
The taste of defeat,
{Bitter it was}
She'd never thought she'd lose,
{She never thought}
Conquered by a hated male,
{A hated male}
Tears of shame fell without control,
{Tears of shame}
If only he had ended her,
{If only he}
If only she wouldn't have survived,
{If only she}
She wouldn't live in shame,
{Live in shame}
She wouldn't feel regret,
{She wouldn't feel}
She really thought it was,

{How foolish}
The end of her sad story,
{How childish}
There is a twist, however,
{A mighty twist}
Fate has rolled the dice,
{Roll of fate}
She never believed such an end for thee,
{Crushed indeed}."

A full moon sat atop the great sky. Pale but strong it was. She remained on the ground, half-conscious, derailed in pain, she waited for her end. However…

Little did she know that her end would be much different from the one she had in mind…her end approached her, and as it did so, the moon shone brighter…

"Playful were her steps,
She was furious, and yet,
She still had a reason to be merry,
Her golden hair shone,
The moonlight was her colour,
She glided under the moonlight,
She approached the misguided one,
The corrupted warrior,
With her spike-shaped flower at hand,
She reached her finally,
The warrior was speechless,
Fear tightly wrapped her body,
She gazed at her coldly,
She was the last sight the warrior saw."

This tale passed into legend. The warrior with the butterfly tattoo was a man of mysteries. Some even say that he was trained by Azure herself, but there was no proof of that being true or not. His battle with the misguided warrior faded from the world; additionally, even fewer people were aware of Azure's involvement in this incident.

Azure became aware of the misguided warrior's actions through her loyal butterflies, for after all, she was the one who gave them life.

The misguided warrior's real name can only be found in the Grand Priest's notes, nowhere else. She was known as a cold-blooded warrior throughout the land, and her existence was eventually considered a myth.

Part Two

Chapter One
The Warrior with
the Butterfly Tattoo

He defeated the 'She-Demon' as they called her, and he headed towards his home where his little girl waited for him. That thought was his only comfort, the fact that he took care of the one major threat that could harm her.

As he walked through the narrow pass up the mountain, butterflies danced around him, beautiful and synchronised they were. He didn't know it yet, but that was the prelude of a visit that would change his life...his and his little girl's.

On his way, he found a wounded soldier, who the moment he was aware of him begged him to finish him off.

The warrior gazed at him with sorrow. He approached the soldier and helped him sit. Then he asked his name.

"For what reason do you want my name, warrior? To simply know the name of the one you eliminated?" he asked the warrior, vexed. The warrior smiled and tended to the wounds of the pained soldier. "What are you doing, warrior, have you gone insane?" the soldier asked in distress.

"You're wounded and you need help, so I'm helping you... I thought that was pretty obvious..." the warrior answered with a chuckle.

"Who are you?!" asked the soldier.

"Ha-ha, you didn't give me your name, and yet you ask for mine, huh?" the warrior laughed. "Very well, my name is Lance, nice to meet you!"

The soldier did not answer; Lance finished tending him and left, never to see the soldier again, not knowing what kind of monster his kindness helped to unleash in the future, and how many souls suffered because of it.

He kept walking up the pathway that would lead home. The butterflies danced around him still; colourful and seemingly ethereal. He noticed a slight difference from the last time he walked the very same pathway. There were lots and lots of flowers in bloom, and that was odd because it wasn't that long ago before he was up there.

There was a breeze, a breeze that slipped through the flowers, causing the flowers to dance with elegance and poise, whilst radiating their colourful beauty; for they were flowers of many colours and shapes.

He resisted the urge to pluck as many flowers as he could from the ground by summoning a lot of willpower, and moved forward, not stopping even for a second.

He then reached his cottage, where his daughter was waiting for him. To his great surprise, his daughter, who had brown hair and big black eyes and was wearing a green dress, had company... It was a golden-haired little girl, who seemed around the same age, and they were playing. Their laughter was genuine and merry, as laughter should be.

Chapter Two
A Merry Golden-Haired Girl, Azure

He approached the little ones and greeted them. His daughter leapt into his arms happily; strangely enough, so did the other one.

"Girls, did you have a good time while I was gone?" he asked them with a smile.

"Yes we did!" they answered with one voice.

"Wonderful! How about we go inside, it's chilly outside… But before that, child, what's your name and where are your parents, may I ask?" he asked the golden-haired girl.

"My name is Azure, sir, and I have no parents, I have none in this world, I am free!" said Azure merrily, and that answer perplexed Lance, the warrior.

"I see, my name is Lance, little Azure. How about I prepare dinner and you can tell us more about you?! I see that you've become fast friends with my daughter, Dawn!" said Lance.

"Yay!" the girls answered with one voice again. They went inside and Lance prepared dinner. The young ones were playing happily. Loud and cheerful voices were resounding in the small flat and it was like spring was already upon them.

Dinner was ready quickly and they ate even quicker. Well, it wasn't much, for they were quite poor, but it was delicious nonetheless; delicious and cosy, and that made all the difference.

Then little Dawn, exhausted from all that playing around, went to sleep. Azure, on the other hand, didn't seem fazed at all, so she stayed. There was a heavy silence when they were left alone.

"You are cautious, warrior Lance, as you should be, after all, we live in dark times now…" said Azure with a surprisingly serious tone.

Lance did not respond. He simply gazed at Azure, waiting to hear more. She laughed merrily, but this time not loudly, for Dawn was fast asleep. She seemed to be a considerate person.

"I understand your hesitation! You just battled a demon! A demon that would've ravaged everything and anything in her wake should you not have interfered!" said Azure merrily.

"How do you know this?" he asked her.

"Well, unlike you, I can travel with other ways besides my feet…in addition to that, I have my butterflies all over to convey news to me!" she answered with the same merry tone, causing a silence again. Lance couldn't find anything to say.

"I love butterflies…" said Lance in the end.

"I'm well aware of that, and they love you in return! They've always talked to me about you! That's why I came to meet you, and I'm really glad that I did!" said she.

"You wanted to meet me? Why?" he asked, filled with curiosity.

"Well, for many reasons!" she answered theatrically. "For starters, I wanted to meet a real father, a father that wholeheartedly loved his daughter; and secondly, I was certain that you could end the misguided she-demon's killing spree!"

That answer raised so many questions for him, but he could only ask one: "How could you possibly know that, you are but a child!" and his reaction caused her laughter once again.

"Appearances can be deceptive, my sweet Lance... I'm older than I look!" said she cryptically. That answer perplexed him even more. "I can see you are puzzled...let's just say that I have something that can make one's dreams a reality; and you should know, you have something similar as well...!" she continued, but seeing confusion expressed on his face she added: "But before we get to that, how about we go outside to continue? There's a beautiful starry sky tonight that I'd like you to see!"

"Very well, let's go outside...but before we do, answer me this, please: do I need to take my sword with me?" he asked Azure frankly, since he could clearly sense her overwhelming spirit force.

"No, my dear Lance, you won't be needing your sword tonight, for I mean you no harm! In fact, I'll become your strongest ally!" said Azure in a serious tone, and a broad smile.

They went outside, after they checked on Dawn, who was now in a deep sleep. They both gazed at the starry sky, and the large moon. Lance loved to gaze at the night sky, and try to count the stars; but the sight he just beheld was the first time he ever saw. It was breathtaking to say the least. The stars covered the entire sky and they were really bright. The moon, usually pale and seemingly wrapped in sorrow, was now bright and merry, like it was aware of Azure's presence.

There they both were, sitting on the swings Lance had made for him and his Dawn. They were now ready to have a more serious conversation, there, under the great starry blue sky.

Chapter Three
Azure's Task, a New Journey Begins

"Do you like it? The stars definitely seem to like you!" said Azure merrily.

"Indeed I do... I simply adore the stars and them shining brightly like that is quite a treat!" said Lance. "But how about we get to the point?"

"Right!" said Azure, and she became serious in an instant. "I was confident that you could defeat the She-Demon 'cause you are her polar opposite!"

"What do you mean? From my research, I've learned that she fought for the memory of her late father. My guess is that along the way, she simply lost her way..." Lance argued.

"That's where you're wrong, my dear and kind-hearted Lance! Her father is very much alive!" said Azure, leaving Lance completely dumbfounded.

"Care to explain?" he asked.

"Indeed I will! Her lineage is somewhat different from what she came to believe, but even so, the family she came to know is alive and well!" Azure started saying playfully, with Lance listening intently. "Her real father is the Grand Priest, however, not the one you are familiar with, but the one that was recently defeated by the five; his brother!"

"I'm not familiar with him…" said Lance.

"Of course not, his legend now only lives in memory, even though it hasn't been that long since he lost to destiny… What's important is, before his downfall, he gave up his children for their own protection. One he gave to a farmer, within his brother's realm, and the other one he sent to a faraway land with his magic. The She-Demon you defeated was the child that remained here!" Azure explained with excitement.

"And she didn't know of all this?" asked Lance.

"No, she did not; but nothing would be different even if she did!" said Azure.

"You can't be certain about that!" Lance argued.

"Up to a certain extent, I certainly can!" Azure answered and chuckled. "I may not use Alchemy to foresee the future, like a certain someone, who I will not even mention now cause I perceive him as a vile, vile man, but I can mostly predict what is to come to be, depending on the situation and the people and beasts who are entangled in it!"

"Please explain!" said Lance.

"With pleasure; should she have learned of her actual lineage, her arrogance would have grown to be even stronger and her hate would've been amplified!" Azure explained.

"True enough…" Lance agreed. "And what of her foster family?"

"The farmer and his wife were working for the Grand Priest you are familiar with, and when she set out on a quest for vengeance they were at his city. Before they left the village to go to work, they had told her that they'll be back as soon as possible, but because she was bitter from being alone and from the Priest's teachings that influenced her village to a massive degree, she projected a story of them being dead and that she had to set out and bring honour to their memory!" said Azure and clapped her hands.

"I see...what a tragedy..." said Lance, with grief dyed in his voice.

"Um, not really! She brought it upon herself!" Azure laughed.

"How can you be so cruel, dear Azure?" Lance asked her with disbelief.

"Simply because I can somehow relate to her, and I can tell you with certainty that cruelty for the sake of cruelty is unbecoming..." Azure explained in a surprisingly serious tone.

"How can you relate to her?" asked Lance, obviously surprised. Azure's face grew dark for the first time.

"Well, some time ago, before I found my dream, my first and most important dream was lost forever..." said Azure bitterly.

"Didn't you try to find it again?" Lance asked with concern.

"I have!" Azure replied strongly and leapt from the swing. "I have been searching for her all this time, but I can't find her anywhere!"

Lance pitied little Azure, for she may seem harsh and cruel, but she actually cares from the bottom of her heart.

"But you know," she started whispering and looked at the stars, "The stars have told me that someday I may meet her again, even if briefly..." as she finished her sentence, some stars rained down from her eyes. Then she sat on the swing again and became her usual merry self.

"I see, you need to simply be patient then!" said Lance.

"Indeed!" she said merrily, "But we digress, our point is not my dreams, but how we can shape yours into reality!"

"But all my dreams are here, and they're very real!" Lance answered simply.

"I hate to be the bearer of bad news, but this place will soon become a rigid wasteland!" said Azure with a sorrowful look.

"How can that happen?" he asked in distress.

"The Grand Priest has amassed too much dark energy and that will draw beings too malevolent to mention...this place will soon become a battlefield of radical forces that only destroy in their wake!" Azure explained.

"Is there a way that we can avoid getting entangled in such a fray?!" Lance asked and looked at his cottage, obviously worrying over little Dawn.

"Indeed there is!" said Azure happily. "That's another reason I came here! I wanted you both to escape this dreadful war!"

"How can it happen?" Lance asked Azure.

"You must flee, and you must do it as soon as possible! And should you choose to do so, I will grant you guidance!" said Azure.

"Can you really–" Lance started saying, but he was abruptly interrupted by the arrival of a dark winged beast; a beast that radiated shadows and looked absolutely menacing, with a long and large tail, sharp teeth and horns, and a grey furry coat. Lance instinctively tried to get to Dawn, but the beast slammed him hard with its tail, knocking him to the back wall. To his great distress, he didn't have his sword with him, so he couldn't protect the little ones. The beast snarled and moved forward; all was lost.

Then, once again, Azure leapt from the swing and faced the monster, but before Lance could utter a word, she started glowing, with a menacing look decorating her face. All the stars reacted to her fury and shine even brighter along with the moon.

"I suggest you leave before you get hurt, you foul creature!" Azure said sternly, who was now wrapped in an ominous light. The creature flinched and flew away in fear. Azure then approached Lance, who was awestruck. She helped him get up. "The nightmare is already upon this place…" said Azure with great sorrow.

"Care to explain this situation?" Lance asked Azure in the end.

"I'm afraid we don't have enough time…if you and my sweet Dawn are to escape, you must do it now!" said Azure and wept. Lance couldn't find the words to comfort her.

"Then how about you wake Dawn while I get ready for the journey?" Lance suggested, and Azure agreed. She went to wake Dawn while Lance wore his armaments. They then tried to explain the situation to Dawn without alarming her.

"Are you coming too, Azure?" Dawn asked, worried.

"No, my sister, I have to follow another route…" said Azure and Dawn wept. Azure embraced her. "Don't you worry, every time you gaze at the stars, you can be certain that I'll look back at you through them! After all, we are sisters now, aren't we?"

"Yes, we are!" answered Dawn and embraced Azure strongly.

"Did you get your treasure, Dawn? You won't be able to come back…" asked Azure, and Dawn immediately started searching her treasure chest. Then Azure turned to Lance and without moving her lips talked to him, directly to his mind: *"I wish we had more time together, the three of us, like a family, but…"* she paused and once again stars rained from her eyes. *"Most importantly, I truly apologise that I'm the bearer of bad news…it seems that I really am a girl that brings misfort–"*

She was interrupted by Lance. He embraced her warmly and said to her in the same way: *"Don't be silly, Azure, thanks to you we will escape, thanks to you we will survive! In my heart, you are like my second daughter, my little Dawn's big sister!"*

Then Dawn came and proudly showed them her treasure. It was a cerulean flower, with round petals. It was the flower that Azure gave her when they met. With this, Dawn and Azure began weeping together, while Lance watched them from above, pained.

"Now, remember to stay hidden and not to stand out too much; at nightfall, travel only if the stars are powerful enough to show you the way. Travel not towards the north, for you might end up in the place where the foul Alchemists had their showdown, the place where they now call: 'the Malicious Kingdom'. Try heading west, where the roads are safer since the threats are currently coming from the east!" said Azure out loud and then she spoke directly into Lance's mind: *"Your only task, my dear Lance, is to hold on tightly to your dream and make sure you never forget it, for your dream, even if it's seemingly gone, it will forever remain close to your heart!"*

Lance kissed Azure on her forehead and they said their goodbyes. The little ones started weeping once again. Then before they departed, Azure said to Dawn: "Try not to do anything rash, okay Dawn?" Dawn agreed with tears in her eyes.

Lance once again embraced Azure and said: "You be careful too, okay Daughter?!" Azure happily agreed. Then they departed, but not one of them could see the stars from above them, where they rained down from the skies with grief for their goodbye…for all three of them, stars were raining down from their eyes…endlessly.

Chapter Four
Heading Westward, the Witch of the Shadows Attacks

Their parting with Azure was indeed tearful, but it was absolutely necessary. Little Dawn wept until her tears ran out, but her father Lance was there for her. They were to travel westward under the guidance of the stars. Lance was vigilant and ready. No new enemy appeared that night as they travelled through the pathways of the hollow mountain.

They climbed down the mountain in just a few hours, despite little Dawn being there, for even though a young one she was, she was able to comprehend the danger up to some level.

Lance was aware of a forest on the other side of the mountain and he figured they could rest there for a few hours, until the little one was ready to travel again. They reached the forest and he prepared a small camp quickly.

He prepared something for them to eat, mainly forest fruits and herbs. After they'd eaten, they rested under the protection of the outer trees of the forest. He didn't want to venture deeper into it, for he had never explored the forest, and therefore he didn't know of the dangers that loomed within it; so he wanted to stay as close to the starlight as possible, just in case.

How right he was…

He wasn't deeply asleep. He woke up in distress from a sudden pierce of danger that went straight through his heart…little Dawn wasn't there with him. He grabbed his sword and began tracking at once. His heart fell into despair, for there were no tracks, it was like she never left.

He, then, inhaled deeply and braced himself. He then asked himself: "What if this is not real?" Then, he suddenly woke up, finding himself bound by thorny vines. It was painful.

He unsheathed his sword to cut the vines, and hurt himself a little bit more in the process. After he was free, he rose up, furious. He then found the tracks he couldn't find while he was under the trance. They were clear as day.

He followed little Dawn's footsteps with haste, ignoring the pain caused by the thorns. He figured the thorns weren't poisonous, for he could normally feel the pain, but just in case he consumed a juice he had made from some of the herbs; those herbs had amazing healing effects, effects mainly for poison.

The tracks led deeper into the forest, and as much as he hated leaving the starry sky, he knew that he didn't have much of a choice in the matter…he had to find Dawn.

As he ventured deeper and deeper into the forest, he saw weird-looking flowers growing there. Not only was their shape disoriented, but they were actually wrapped in shadows. He ignored their calling, and moved forward with determination and bravery. Then suddenly:

"Go away, leave us alone!" a whisper was carried with the wind.

"Oh no, I won't!" Lance answered in the same tone, this time with the wind carrying his words to the one that warned him.

There wasn't anything else. Lance was angrier than ever. He reached his destination, it was a clearing where a woman with long red hair sat on the grass, surrounded by the same type of flowers he saw on his way.

There she was as well, Dawn. Behind the woman, wrapped in vines, she didn't touch the ground; she was much higher from it, in fact…seemingly fast asleep, but he knew better now, she was in a trance.

"What do you want with my daughter?" Lance asked coldly. "Release her at once!"

"No, she's my daughter now!" she answered and turned to face him. She was pale and beautiful, but in her large grey eyes there was nothing, they seemed completely empty. She radiated a level of insanity Lance had never encountered before.

"I see…brace yourself, witch!" Lance said and unsheathed his sword. "I will save my daughter whether you like it, or not!"

She smiled and jumped up. Then vines encircled Lance, but with swift swings of his sword, he cut them all. Then he leapt towards her, in order to strike.

She barely managed to escape his wrath. Then in distress, she did something that even she didn't think she'd do…the vines that entangled Dawn started to tighten their grip.

He stopped moving. She started screaming, saying that it's his fault for that. Then almost immediately, vines encircled him. He knew that he only had one shot at this. He allowed the vines to tangle around him. As they did, he closed his eyes and visualised the situation.

He then sensed the witch's guard, it was down. At that very instant, he cut the vines with one fell swoop and attacked her relentlessly. He got one clear strike, which was more than enough. She screamed in distress, then the shadows enveloped her and she was gone with a massive explosion of thick shadows.

Lance was victorious. Hastily he caught Dawn as she fell, for the witch's spell was undone. Dawn opened her eyes and said:

"Daddy, where are we?" she obviously had no memory of what had taken place there. Lance rejoiced. Those memories weren't memories a child should carry… "Daddy, what's wrong with your sword?" she then asked in awe.

On Lance's sword now appeared a scribbling. On the blade bright blue letters spelled: 'MASTER OF THE RAINBOW'.

Chapter Five
The Master Blacksmith,
Alexandrea the Wildfire

The witch was gone, but the shadows still loomed. Lance held little Dawn on his one arm, sheathed his sword with the other, and hastily made his way out of the forest.

It was already dawn, but the sun couldn't make it through the decay of the forest trees. It was as though a sickness was planted there, a sickness that would only grow as time passed. They left behind the forest as quickly as possible, never to go there together again.

After they walked for a while, they stopped for a little bit. It was time for lunch; Lance still had some fruits in his bag, but after they ate them, little Dawn had a surprise for him...

She took out a flower from her shoulder bag. It was a flower like the ones from the forest. A shadow flower it was. She must've picked it up while she was in a trance, for she had no recollection as to why it was in her bag. The temptation for those flowers was that strong even in a trance, apparently...

She was excited about it; and how could she not be? She was young and blissfully unaware of the dangers those flowers had in store for their holders; and most importantly, let's be realistic about it, the flower was simply gorgeous and quite mysterious.

"So I take it, you want to keep it?" he asked Dawn.

"Yes Daddy! I don't know how I got it, but look how beautiful it is…" Dawn answered anxiously.

Lance couldn't bear the thought of taking that happiness away from his little girl, so he caved and thus, starting a chain of events that will affect many souls in the future, peoples' and animals' alike.

They were now at the outskirts of a small village, a village that had no name. The people there stayed inside, never leaving, and they rarely allowed an outsider to enter. In that village, it was rumoured that a renowned blacksmith resided, so Lance figured it was a good idea to consult that blacksmith about the new twist his sword had in store for him.

Luckily for him, the blacksmith was easier to find than he originally thought. On the outskirts of the village, long before entering, there was a large hut where a tall woman was sitting on a chair, reading a scroll.

"Excuse me miss, could you please help me find someone?" Lance asked her politely, and his Dawn bowed gracefully. The woman glanced at them and smiled.

"And who is it the one you're searching for, may I ask?" she replied politely, but something menacing was hidden behind her words.

"I'm searching for a rumour, actually, about an incredibly skilled blacksmith…it's been said that he lives in the village ahead," said Lance.

"I see…" she said and sighed. She, then, got up and gave Lance a fiery glance. "I'm afraid there is no male blacksmith in the village ahead…your search is in vain!"

"Then maybe the blacksmith is a woman, it makes no difference to me…a person's sex isn't definitive about one's profession; a person's soul is what makes all the difference!" said Lance softly.

"Pretty words you speak of, strangers, but I can't help wondering whether you truly believe them or not…!" she laughed.

"Try me!" Lance challenged her, making her laugh even harder.

"Very well…" she said and picked up a lance that was near her. "I can tell that you are an experienced swordsman… So my question is this: would you fight seriously against me, a woman?!"

"If it's a duel you want, then so be it! But if you don't mind, I wouldn't want my daughter to be present in this duel!" said he and Dawn reacted instantly. But before little Dawn could say anything…

"I agree!" she said. "Children should be protected from battle and anguish!"

"No, Daddy, I want to watch!" Dawn retaliated, she couldn't keep it in any longer; and when she saw her father trying to say something else, she continued: "A duel between warriors isn't necessarily a battle to the bitter end, right?! I really want to watch you battle!"

Lance was reluctant, but the woman laughed.

"She really is the daughter of a warrior! If you're game, warrior, I am too! She can stay and observe if she so desires!" she said.

Lance didn't want his Dawn to watch, but if he wouldn't let her spectate the duel, he'd have a much bigger problem later…

"Very well, but you are to watch from a safe distance and you are absolutely forbidden to interfere under any circumstances, am I clear?" Lance explained the rules, and Dawn happily agreed.

Then they got ready. The duel started with Dawn's signal. It was wicked! The woman was a true warrior. All her swings were swift and true, however, Lance wasn't a pushover either. He held his own, gracefully.

They both struggled. Each of them almost received hits more than twice. Lance was really serious about it. He figured the only way to win was to utilise his extended experience on duelling. She was an expert on using a lance, true, but it was obvious to him that she wasn't used to battling like he was. He used his footwork to disorient her, and thanks to that move he managed to beat her, without drawing a single drop of blood; he simply tripped her with a graceful kick. Dawn rejoiced.

"I'm beaten…" she said, trying to catch her breath.

"Just barely…" said Lance in the same manner.

"You really were serious about this duel, huh?!" she asked.

"I'd be dead if I wasn't…" he answered simply. "You are a true warrior, my dear, but fortunately for me, you lack battle experience!"

"Well, I am forging them, and then practising, but I do it on my own, I don't have an opponent…" she said and then she burst into laughter. "Indeed, I am the blacksmith that you're searching for…" she continued after seeing their shocked expressions on their faces. "My name is Alexandrea!"

"Very nice to meet you, Alexandrea, my name is Lance and this is my daughter Dawn!" Lance introduced themselves with high honour. "But how about we continue our conversation someplace comfortable and most importantly without weapons…?"

"I agree! Let's go inside and have the conversation you're so eager to have… I have a feeling it's about that sword of yours…" said she and chuckled; "Oh, don't look so surprised, it's my job to know about these things!" she added after seeing his surprise about her assessment.

Then they entered the hut, all three of them. Alexandrea boiled some herbal leaves for them to sip while they had their conversation. The herbal leaves' scent was so pleasant and calming, and they were feeling happy and relaxed by simply breathing it. It was almost time…

Chapter Six
The Legendary Moon Sword

They made themselves comfortable inside the hut. It was cosy, small but adorable. There were many, many weapons inside, but most of them for decoration on the walls. Alexandrea served them the herbal drinks she just made.

"Now, give me your sword, please!" said Alexandrea politely. Lance gave her the sword. It was sheathed, but upon touching it, she was overwhelmed by its power. "This is truly a unique sword..." she said and unsheathed it. She gasped in wonder. "Your sword has seen many battles, in all of which, you must've reigned victorious..."

"How can you tell?!" he asked anxiously.

"The very fact that it evolved tells me so!" answered her; "These engraved writings weren't here before, correct?!"

Lance was at a loss for words. She figured all this out on her own, without the slightest information. If with a single examination she could tell this much, who knows what else she's capable of...

"What can you tell me about this?" he asked in the end.

"Not much, I'm afraid... You see, your sword evolved, yes, but not to its final stage!" she replied.

"You mean to say there is still room for growth?" he asked.

"Indeed, for both you and your sword!" she answered happily.

"What can I do to help it evolve?" Lance asked anxiously.

"That is not something I can answer with certainty…from what I can tell is that your sword is waiting for something…" she said and sighed.

"Like what?" he asked.

"I cannot tell, but it's clear to me that it wants to evolve too!" she replied and gave him back his sword.

"I see…" said Lance, and the moment he grasped the hilt of his sword, the engraved letters lit up, bright and blue.

"Now that's a beautiful bond… I can clearly see that your sword is more than happy to be wielded by you!" said Alexandrea, lost in awe. "What about you little one, will you become a warrior like your daddy when you grow up?"

"Me? No, I don't want to be a warrior, I want to be a star!" said Dawn filled with excitement.

"A star? What do you mean?" asked Alexandrea, perplexed.

"Well, you see, I want to shine the road for everyone; that way no one will get lost!" answered Dawn.

"I see!" said Alexandrea and smiled. "Now that's a wonderful dream, sweetie!"

"Thank you very much! If I can work hard enough, I know I can achieve it!" said Dawn, brimming with excitement.

"Apparently, both Father and Daughter are filled with untapped latent powers…" Alexandrea thought. "Both of them have a shining future ahead of them, one way or another…"

After their conversation, they said their goodbyes and left Alexandrea's hut. Lance didn't know it yet, but he'd definitely meet her again, for their pathways were meant to intertwine for many, many times. Alexandrea embraced little Dawn warmly before they left, and gave her a beautiful set of bracelets that were made of round-shaped pink petals.

Lance figured they should head a little bit northwest this time, that way they could even make it to a place that was said everything was made out of crystal. That possibility made little Dawn really happy; and with these thoughts in mind, they were headed towards more adventures, with the sun smiling from above them, not knowing that heartache was right around the corner, waiting…

Chapter Seven
The Shadow Returns, a New Star is Added to the Sky

They travelled northwest, after they parted ways with Alexandrea. Lance was somewhat satisfied from what he had learned, but he still wanted to learn more, and that made him a little bit anxious. Little Dawn, on the other hand, was completely enthusiastic and sad simultaneously, about their last meeting and parting.

Dawn was really happy that she was able to express her wonderful dream to her father, after all, it was a dream that was born after she met with Azure, who at that point was like an older sister…if she could become a star, she'd be able to light Azure's way to find the one dream that still eludes her…

"Daddy, what is your dream?" Dawn asked Lance.

"My dream? Well, sweetheart, my dream is you!" Lance answered with a smile.

"Come on, Daddy, tell me! You must have a dream that you can't wait to make it a reality!" Dawn nagged him.

"One day, when you're older, you'll know what I'm talking about…" said Lance with a chuckle.

"What about Mum? Do you want to find her?" Dawn asked.

"Someday, I'm sure we'll meet her again…" said Lance slowly.

"What happened to her?" asked Dawn.

"She had to chase her dream, darling, she's out and about in this vast world we live in!" answered Lance with a smile. "Your mum is an adventurer; the entire world is calling her…she was really sad when she left you behind, but I'm sure that someday, we'll meet her again, and you can ask her anything you want!"

"Does she love us?" Dawn asked anxiously.

"Indeed she does," Lance answered simply, and with that simple answer, Dawn was overjoyed; for after all, they didn't talk much about her mother, and hearing that she loved them was a harbinger of sheer joy.

They walked in silence afterwards. Dawn was skipping happily, and that happiness was making Lance feel complete…little did he know that the worst had yet to be revealed…

They had arrived at a place Lance had travelled to in one of his past expeditions. It was a valley that one could walk through in only one hour if one were hasty; so Lance figured that in an hour or so they could make it. The day was almost over, but if they hurried, they would be one step closer to their destination, wherever that was… They would only have to be swift.

They walked hastily. Dawn was aware of the danger, so she walked close to her father. An hour of intense walking passed and they could finally see the pathway that led out of the valley. They rejoiced, but that happiness didn't last…

Suddenly a shadow passed over them, and blocked their path. It was the same ghastly winged beast that attacked them at their flat on the mountain. What happened next, even Lance couldn't stop…

The beast unleashed two radical crimson red rays by flapping its wings hard. Lance threw his body in front of Dawn to protect her, but she wouldn't have it, and with unwitting speed, far beyond her year or training, she shielded her dear daddy with her body.

As she took the full force of the beast's attacks, her body dispersed into countless orbs of brilliant light and headed towards the sky, leaving Lance behind, whilst still trying to comprehend what had just happened…

The beast snarled, filled with pleasure and excitement from its new accomplishment. That, of course, was about to be cut short…

Lance released a massive cry. Then, filled with fury, he unsheathed his sword, which was now luminous, and he dashed towards the beast. The beast once again unleashed an attack, an attack that Lance deflected with his sword, and as he did so, the beast was blinded by the sword's radiance and flinched, making the sight of Lance's fury the last picture it saw in that world…

Lance leapt and slew the beast with one swift and powerful swing. After the attack, the beast caught fire and turned into dust. Then Lance fell onto his knees and wept. He had just lost the only glimmer of light from his life. He couldn't bring himself to look at the sky, where his daughter was now. He could only face the ground, where his tears fell.

A strong breeze scattered the beast's ashes everywhere, but Lance didn't notice. He couldn't notice how beautiful the sky had become as dusk was upon him, either. Then, as he wept, a very familiar voice resounded through the wind:

"I love you, Daddy, please don't cry! I'll always love and watch from here…from the stars!"

Lance couldn't stop his tears, even after his daughter's plea. He could only think of one thing: how he'd find the root of the problem and solve it; basically, who let loose those monsters and most importantly how to stop them…

He got up and picked his sword from the ground, where he threw it earlier, as he fell onto his knees. As he was about to sheathe it, he noticed some changes…the colours of the letters that spelled: 'Master of the Rainbow' had a million colours, instead of only blue. It was as if he had become the master of the rainbow now, the rainbow of feelings that could stretch all the way from happiness down to sadness in one go.

He sheathed his sword and decided to change direction. Since his Dawn wasn't with him anymore, going to the place where everything was made out of crystal wasn't a priority…his next destination would be the cursed kingdom Azure had mentioned. There, where the epic battle between the alchemists had taken place. It's been said that after that battle, there was malice all over, malice that never slept…the kingdom that was called 'Malicious' by the world… Maybe over there, he'd be able to find some answers…

He walked towards that kingdom with a void in his heart, a void that would never be filled in this lifetime, but thanks to that void, he'd be protected by dangers that still haven't appeared before him, dangers he's still unaware of…

The sky was now dark, like his thoughts. His pain was like clouds in the sky, hiding the light, but regardless of the intense pain, he didn't stop walking, the same way he didn't stop weeping…

The Lady Dressed in September

Recollections of a troubled mind.

"How long has it been here? A long time, I'm sure; it feels like eternity. I know I was at fault at the time, but I won't let it haunt me forever. I have to break free. I have to break out and live again. I missed dreaming and striving to bring those dreams into reality."

To be honest, I am aware that on some level I am at fault, but still, I can't stomach this. I don't want to be imprisoned. I don't want to be confined. I don't want to be limited.

I will calm myself down, and I will reflect on what I've done and come out of this ordeal stronger…but before that, I should start preparing for my way out.

Chapter One
Vs the Illusionist Faceless Mage

I still don't know how long it has been. I'm afraid to even count. The startling part is that even though I am alone here, I hear whispers all around and I have no idea who or what is causing them.

I became obsessed with finding out who that was. To my great surprise, my powers were to some extent still active, so I could bend the space of this place and traverse into the real world.

I found out who it was quite easily; after all, that person wasn't trying to conceal himself. With my mind's eye, I was able to see who it was, sort of. He was seemingly a faceless mage, and I could sense a great deal of dark power resonating from within him.

"You found me…" he whispered.

I didn't answer. He hurt me. I became enraged and bent my will to strike back. I felt him hurting, and that was quite invigorating.

"You dare to challenge me, you insolent pup?" he whispered manically.

I laughed and once again attacked him. I loved every second of it. "You will be the first!" I thought and kept on damaging him. He then struck back. I felt hurt, but it only made me feel stronger.

Feeling confident enough, he started using his special powers of illusion. I felt the pressure and the anguish. He was no joke, indeed…a real illusionist mage!

Our battle kept on going for long, although I don't know for how long exactly. It felt like an eternity of hurt and despair. At last, I felt him crack under the pressure, my pressure. I reigned victorious in the battle against him, but I was somewhat aware that it was not the end of him. I somehow knew that I'd meet him again someday.

"You might've been my first, but you certainly won't be my last…" I thought and lost myself in a vortex born out of my own powers.

Chapter Two
Black Alchemy

I came after a while; I don't know for how long I was out. I felt stronger, like the battle with the faceless mage empowered me. I knew it wasn't enough, though. I need more power if I am to escape this prison. I figured that, like before, I could traverse into the real world through my willpower alone; and I was right.

Once again, I bent my will on escaping, and I was successful. I did find myself in a kingdom that must've been far away from the woods I used to live in.

The kingdom seemed dark and full of decay. I traversed through it, and what I saw somewhat frightened me. All over the place, there were remnants of a power I had never seen before. It was a lot different than the power the Ethereal Flowers were letting on...it felt like the entire kingdom was cursed.

The more I lingered, the greater my fear grew. The source of all that power was hidden from me, as if someone was aware of my presence and was leading me astray every time I was getting close...

And then...

"I see you started to get the hang of it, huh?" a male voice resounded in my mind. At that point, I felt my entire being grow cold; I could not respond. "There's no need to fear me, my dear, I mean you no harm!" he said, and I immediately felt better.

"Who are you?" I asked.

"Who, me? I am but a humble Alchemist who, like you, is currently imprisoned," answered he in a nonchalant tone.

"You're imprisoned and you don't care?!" I asked in shock.

"Why should I care? My time will soon come, once again! So there's no need to worry…" he answered simply.

"I wish I could be like that too…" I said with a melancholy tone.

"If that is your wish, I can make it a reality!" he said.

"I can feel that what you're saying is true; however, before I agree to anything, I must ask of the price I have to pay to make it happen…" I replied.

"Price? Did I say there'd be a price? There's no price! You can say that I'll do it just for fun, simply to see what happens…" said he while laughing.

I couldn't tell whether he was serious or not… I decided to take my chances and trust him for the time being.

"Very well then, I accept your proposal, but how do you think I'll escape this prison?" said I, trying to imitate his nonchalant attitude.

"Well, the first step is to make your wish come true. You must find a Zen-like state and learn that, however large and intense a problem is, a solution can be found, even later down the line…" answered he.

"I'm not sure I understand..." I said, utterly perplexed by his answer.

"Well, let me put it this way, you found yourself in this prison because you were blinded by pride and rage, completely ignoring the warning signs and making all the mistakes you never should've made!" he began explaining, making my heart shrink... "But if you were calm and more prepared, you'd still be the ruler of that dump you wanted to call home, understand?"

"So it's all about preparation and keeping my cool?" I asked, beginning to grasp his point.

"Well, not all about, but these two factors are the start if you really want to escape the prison you are currently trapped in..." he answered.

"Is there something special about this particular prison?" I asked, all intrigued.

"Indeed, there is! You see, the prison you're in now, has been created by a very special Ethereal Flower that can be found in that dump of yours...how did you live there, anyway?" he sighed and continued, "And from what I see, the one that imprisoned you, used three of those pink nightmares, which means there are three layers through which you need to break if you want to free yourself, and all three have different colours!"

So much information, all at once, and even though I had so many questions, only one actually came through.

"What do you mean they are all different colours?" I asked seriously, trying to hide my eagerness.

"Hm, that's good, you've already started to mature!" said he, satisfied. "Well, you see, because three of the pink nightmares were used on you, three kinds of defence mechanisms have been created, all of them to prevent you from escaping!" he explained.

"Is there a way to destroy them, or even to bypass them?" I asked hastily.

"Indeed there is, but to do so, you'll have to deceive and cause hurt at will, but that's not really a problem for you, is it?" he laughed.

"No, it is not!" said I, brimming with confidence... Finally, a way out!

"Wonderful then. I could tell you exactly what to do, but that's not fun, so I'll tell you only where to start!" said he, and I celebrated. "Before telling you, however, I must give you some other information that I'm positive you'll need along the way!"

I gasped and once again felt completely overwhelmed.

"The power you feel around this entire kingdom is Alchemy, and to be more accurate, Black Alchemy. Later down the line, you will definitely encounter beings that can wield it, not the Black Alchemy, but two of the four kinds of Alchemy. You see, the Black Alchemy was used by a monster long ago, and the Gold Alchemy, by the Crimson Alchemist, who is long dead. The two kinds you will encounter are the dark and white Alchemies! And be warned, even in your astral state, they can still cause you harm! Your first task is to go and defeat the Witch of the Greenfields, it's been said that she rivals the power of the Witch of the Black Forest! Succeed and you will be able to obtain the clue for your next task! I'm so looking forward to meeting you in person... 'Till then, ta-ta!" he concluded, and before I was able to respond, I lost myself in a white vortex.

Chapter Three
Vs the Witch of the Greenfields

When I finally came to, I didn't know if talking to that man actually happened, or if it was all a figment of my imagination. I chose to believe it was real and to pursue the path he talked about, for I really wanted to escape this place, and if that meant I needed more power to do so, then so be it.

According to him, I am to find the Witch of the Greenfields and defeat her in order to find the next clue. In all honesty, that sounded simple enough; after all, winning is what I do!

So once again I bent the space around me and in my astral form, I traversed into the real world. Surprisingly enough, it took me a while to find her. There were so many entities with high-level spiritual presence and I had to try really hard to distinguish which one she was. I figured that she'd be the one that would make me feel nauseous.

When I approached her, she immediately sensed my presence. She may have had closed eyes, but I could feel her glance on me already.

"Well, well, well…" she said and opened her eyes. She then laid on a bed of flowers. "And who might you be?" she asked, somewhat intrigued.

"My name does not matter," I replied.

"Well, of course it does! If you don't give me your name, why should I give you mine?" she wondered aloud, without a care in the world.

"I see, well, I have long since forgotten my real name, and the name of my choosing doesn't matter anymore…and to be honest, for what I am to do now, your name is of no importance…" I sighed.

"I see…and what are you here to do, then?" she asked softly.

"I am here to defeat you!" I answered simply.

"I see…" she smiled, "Let's get on with it, then!" she said and got up slowly.

I attempted to make the first move, but I found myself frozen from fear.

"If you don't make a move, I think I will!" she said, and in that instant, I felt an unbelievable amount of pain. A pain that lasted for eternity, but it was actually only one second. This feeling I experienced was like the one I felt back then, in my premonition, but at that time, it didn't actually hurt… "Come on, sweetie, you have to move, for if this keeps up, you'll die!" said she, all concerned.

But I couldn't find the strength to make any move, not even speak… She sighed and once again I found myself covered with intense pain, so much of it that I couldn't stand anymore. I fell onto my knees, not able to get up again. I was defeated, effortlessly.

"I didn't enjoy this fight, sweetie...hopefully, next time, you'll be able to muster your fear and actually put up a fight, okay?!" said she, and with a wave of her hand, opened up a massive white vortex, and I found myself back in my prison before I lost myself into the hurt and passed out.

Chapter Four
Visit to the Witch of the Black Forest

When I came to, my fear was long gone, but the clue for what my next move should be was clear as the blue skies to me. I had to conquer my fear, and the person who could help me has to be the Witch of the Black Forest; otherwise, why would he mention her?

Once again, I exercised my will to bend the space around me. This time, however, I struggled to do so. Fortunately, I was able to locate her pretty easily. She emanated the most sinister spiritual presence I ever encountered. But this time, the entrance was shut. I couldn't get through; it was like the Witch herself was blocking my way.

It felt impossible, but I didn't give up. I struggled greatly, but with no effect. She was too powerful for me. Then, her voice resounded in my head: "Go away, child! You reek of fear and ignorance!"

I ignored her and kept on trying to enter her forest. She hurt me. But that didn't stop me either. I persisted greatly. She was my only hope. I had to succeed.

"Why do you persist, child? You very well know that I have the power to end you, even in the form you have assumed right now... I'm sure he told you this!" said she angrily and hurt me again.

"I won't give up!" I murmured. "You're my only hope to conquer my fear!" In a matter of moments, the pain stopped, and I was allowed entry. I saw her standing tall, welcoming me into her forest, the legendary Black Forest of Nightmares, the forest that was said to rival the Golden Woods of old, in stature and power.

"Explain yourself, child!" she bid me.

"I recently suffered a crushing defeat from the Witch of the Greenfields–" I started saying, but I was interrupted by a mocking laughter.

"I'm aware of that, child! Is that all?" she patronised me.

"No, but after a discussion I had with a certain individual, I was told that I'd get a clue of what my next move should be after I defeated her..." I explained.

"And?! What was the clue, aside from suffering a humiliating defeat?" asked her with disgust.

"Well, that was the reason behind my defeat!" I answered. "I was utterly defeated because an old fear awakened from deep inside me when I faced her, and I'm confident that if I am to escape the prison I am trapped in, I need to conquer that fear and become stronger by doing so!"

"Indeed, child! If one is to become stronger, conquering one's fear is a prerequisite!" said she, with an obvious change in her tone. "You're in luck, child! You are in the perfect place to do that!"

"Really? How so?" I asked eagerly.

"Your question comes as no surprise, child. After all, even though you yourself used to live in a legendary forest, you knew very little about it..." she explained, leaving me speechless. "You see, child, this forest is unique; by venturing ever deeper to its core, one is able to face one's deepest fears...you could say that it grants the traveller the chance to face the problem at its root!"

"So I am to venture there and by doing so I'll be able to conquer my fear?" I asked.

"Simply put, yes, but it's not that simple...if you're not able to do it, there's a chance to lose oneself and become a permanent resident here, forever!" she answered simply. "Are you sure you want to go through with it?"

"I am, yes, I am willing to go the distance if that means that I'll finally be free! I'll do whatever it takes!" I replied instantly.

"Wonderful, then!" she laughed. "Now, go!" she then waved her hand, and the vines behind her opened a pathway. "Be warned, child! The root of your fear is not just one, but two! Do not stop until you resolve both of them; otherwise, you'll never be free of them, and your entire ordeal will be for naught!" She then disappeared with a dark flash, and her voice resounded: "Good luck! If you are successful, you will definitely see me again!"

I, then, boldly moved forward into the dark and thorny pathway that led to the forest's core.

Chapter Five
Tackling the Past

Walking down that road reminded me of my own home, back in the woods. Every time I ventured towards the core, I felt timid and never actually went through with it. But this time was different, I had to be brave and move forward, for how will I ever be able to return to my home, if I don't have the strength to do so?

As I walked, my anxiety rose rapidly, so much that I heard my heartbeat clearly. Lost spirits appeared and started closing in on me, but surprisingly enough, I felt compassion radiating from them, rather than hostile intentions. They felt like my allies, rather than my enemies.

I finally reached a well, and all of a sudden, I felt thirsty. I wasn't aware that I could feel thirst in this form… I leaned over to drink, without thinking. Suddenly, a pair of young hands pulled me in. I hit the water hard and all of a sudden, memories started to flood. I saw myself playing with a younger girl in a meadow. I can clearly remember her now, for some reason…she was my sister, before I got lost and forgotten. We were so happy together.

I remember. How much I loved her, how much I felt the need to protect her. Just seeing her golden hair and bright eyes again caused my heart to ache. The pain was really unbearable.

However, it didn't stop there…

My younger self and my little sister then lay down on the grass and talked.

"Azure, will you ever forget me?" my younger self asked.

"You are my sister!" Azure laughed. "I'll never forget you!" she answered happily, making my younger self laugh merrily.

I couldn't take it. I fell onto my knees and wept. The pain now was like death creeping in my heart. How could she forget me?! She promised she wouldn't!

My tears could not stop. The young girls in my memory laughed together, while I wept on my knees, shaking hard. At first, my grief wouldn't let me hear it…

But then…

"I never forgot about you, silly!" a faint voice resounded over and over again.

At last! I heard it, and the pain stopped instantly. I don't think I ever really cared that my parents forgot about me…the real reason behind all of this heartache originated from the single thought of my sister forgetting my very existence!

I don't know how she reached me, but now I have another reason to move forward and obtain the power to escape. I want to see my sister again.

The memory was gone and I found myself on the road again. One thorn that pierced my heart was gone, but another one was still there, causing me intense pain. So I had to keep on going.

I walked and walked, but nothing new happened at first, but suddenly the forest changed and I found myself in a shining palace, with a lord sitting on a grand throne.

"Have you come back for me, child?" the lord asked me, but I didn't reply. He was the same person from my premonition. I felt completely powerless in his presence. I fell onto my knees.

"Who are you?" I asked him, after I gathered enough willpower to do so.

"Me?" The real question is, "Who are YOU, child?" he replied.

"I am the Great Globalea!" I answered and felt power surging through me again.

"No, that's not who you are..." he replied, pained with grief. "The memory you relieved earlier did not depict Globalea and Azure, but rather Mistylea and Azure..."

"Mistylea..." I murmured. My real name was just revealed to me. I felt overwhelmed.

"Who are you, child?" he asked me again.

I didn't answer right away. I simply couldn't find a correct answer. Who am I, really? Doubt gnawed at me, but an answer did come out eventually.

"Who am I, you ask?" I began saying and I rose, like a child learning how to stand. "I am Mistylea, and I am Globalea, and I'll be the lady dressed in starlight and moonlight... I will be whatever I have to be, in order to reunite with my sister! I don't care how long it takes and what kind of powers I have to face, I really don't care! Whatever they are, I'll meet them head on! I will escape and walk into the real world again!"

The lord sighed and rose. It was a sight to behold. Powerful is not enough to measure up his greatness. "Then you'll have to face me, and you'll have to win, if that's what you really want!"

As our eyes met, I felt his overwhelming power. As I looked at him deep in his eyes, one thing was painfully clear to me.

"No…" I answered. "I have no hope of victory against an opponent like you… I am much weaker than you…"

He then laughed and sat down comfortably on his throne again. "Well done, child!" he said softly, making tears run through my eyes. I was fully perplexed. "You see, dear child, I was never the root of your fear. It was the thought of your sister and your inability to accept your weaknesses… Now, if you really want to gain the power to walk once again into the real world and reunite with your sister, by all means, do it! And when you're ready to come and meet me again, I'll be here, patiently waiting for your arrival!" said he merrily and then snapped his fingers; I found myself back in the forest with the Witch smiling at me. I was successful.

Chapter Six
The Journey into
the Land of Mystics

"How do you feel, child?" the Witch asked me with a smile. I didn't answer right away, for even I didn't know exactly how I felt.

"To be honest… I don't really know…" I mumbled after a while. She laughed, but not with scorn; it was actually a pleasant laugh.

"That's to be expected; his majesty himself just explained everything to you!" she said, still laughing.

"You know him?" I asked her eagerly.

"Well of course I know him!" she exclaimed loudly. "But what's really surprising is that a young child like you actually had an audience with him…and what's more, not only once, but twice!"

"Who is he?" I asked in shock.

"Who? Well, he is one of the cornerstones of the world…at least the world of the in-between! One could say that he governs the world and all those that wield any source of power!" she explained.

"That means that he's even more powerful than you?" I asked, causing her to laugh even louder than before.

"He's more powerful than everyone, child!" she said. "He's always sitting on his throne, ever watchful of the events happening in this and in any world!"

"I see…" I said, lost in thought.

"Now, can you try again and tell me how you feel?" she asked me once more.

"I feel…at peace! Like I know full well what I have to do!" I answered with a gentle sigh.

"Wonderful, then; that means you are ready to continue your journey through this vast world!" she said merrily. "But to do that, you need to know where to go next and who you have to defeat if you are to be successful in your quest! Hm?" She stopped talking after she saw the expression on my face. "I know what you are thinking…or should I say who?" she laughed. "You needn't worry about him, child; he can take care of himself, for after all, in terms of power, he's considered to be on an equal level of power as his majesty!"

I was lost in awe. No wonder he was able to guide me through all of this so efficiently. "Where should I go next, then?" I asked in the end.

"You must travel to a small island, south of Tempestea Island, the island of the Mystics, and you must take down their leader. If you manage to defeat him, you'll be one step closer to your goal. But be warned, child; he's not an opponent one can take down by sheer force…you must use creative ways of battle if you are to defeat him!" said she, and once again vanished with a brilliant flash.

I was left all alone in the woods, but now they didn't seem menacing; in fact, they reminded me of home, the woods I used to live in. I even started to miss the villagers, whom I wronged.

With those gentle thoughts in mind, I focused once again and, in my astral form, I journeyed through the world. I found Tempestea Island and then headed south. I found the island of the Mystics. I was ready to start my new ordeal.

The island I found myself on was a mess. A mess from every angle. Residual energies were all over the place; but that's not all, they were all tethered with intense hate. Although this was nothing compared with the hatred and resentment I sensed in the kingdom I met him...

I followed the hate and it led me to a really vile man. He didn't sense me right away, and that was comforting! He wasn't as powerful as I feared he'd be.

"Who are you, and why are you here?" he asked suddenly. Rude I know, but my fear and anxiety were long gone, so I played.

"Who am I? You could say that I am your friend!" I answered slowly.

"I don't desire friends!" he answered angrily.

"Then what is it you desire?" I asked in return.

"And why should I tell you?" he mocked me.

"Why, you ask? Because I can be of help!" I answered softly.

He didn't reply right away. He took his time to think about it first. "Fine, but if you can't help me, your life is forfeit!" he answered strongly.

"Wonderful, I accept those terms. Now, tell me more of your desires!" I said slowly out loud, and celebrated strongly from within.

"Well…" he hesitated for a moment. "I want to reign supreme… I want everything and anything to fall into ruin… I want complete and utter annihilation!" said he like a child expressing some new thoughts.

I didn't reply. To me, his moronic desires were a good thing. Thanks to them, I'd be able to manipulate him easily. But my pause caused him anxiety, and he started screaming.

"There's no need to be upset, my cute little friend… I was simply trying to comprehend the brilliance of your desires!" I said slowly.

"Really?" He asked like a toddler.

"Indeed! And I'm sure that I can help you to make at least one a reality!" I said merrily.

"Then what are we waiting for? Let's begin!" said he eagerly.

"Indeed we should!" I replied, and dark schemes had already begun forming in my mind, schemes that would ensure his downfall and my uprise.

Chapter Seven
Weaving the Threads of Destiny

I stayed for a while with that vile man, named Antichoos, being his private advisor, visible only to him. In that time, I learned a lot about Mystics and their craft. Apparently, they tapped on the earth's power through meditation, but I knew there was more to it than that, so I kept on digging.

Antichoos was so pleased with my councils that he even explained to me the ranks of the Mystics without me asking. He was the grand Mystic, standing above everyone else, and the rest were inconsequential. His son was to take the reins when he was ready. He was a ruthless tyrant, never approaching anything else than him. The only one he could even tolerate was his son, Echidnos, and even him barely.

Thanks to that, however, my job became even easier, for even though he was suspicious of me at first, he then wholeheartedly trusted in me and my councils. It was clear to me, at my current level of power I'd lose if I were to challenge him; but if I were to use that trust and manipulate him, I'd be able to work wonders. For example, I really came to dislike the Mystics, and it would be really nice if they were to…disappear!

As my second move, well the first one was to gain his trust, I decided to fuel his ego and plant a deeper discord into his heart. Fortunately, that was pretty easy; he quickly distrusted everyone around him even more than before, and found solace only in me. In fact, he even started calling me a nickname that came to be by my moody attitude and the dress I imagined my astral form wearing…he called me: The Lady Dressed in September…figures!

The rest of his men thought that he started to go insane, since they weren't able to see me, and they in return began distrusting him as well. Soon, the Lady Dressed in September was feared and hated by all Mystics.

After I planted my seeds of discord to all Mystics, it was time for my next move: to take down Antichoos. I thought that it'd be fun if I ended his lineage before taking him down.

In my time there, I learned of an old mystic ritual that was created by an alchemist of the previous era. Supposedly it would summon a great deal of power in exchange for the caster's life force; but it could be used in another way, the caster could draw the life force of everything around him.

Naturally, that was the way to go. I fuelled his ego into casting that very spell in order to immortalise himself. He had learned all the legends about a dark Alchemist, who it's been said that he defeated the Alchemist that created that spell, and actually motivated him into casting it.

Guided by my councils, he decided to prepare the ritual deep underground, where no prying eye can watch his greatness. My greatest joy came when one of my sneaky whispers bloomed inside him. I suggested to him that if he wanted to be truly immortal, it would be wise to use his son in the ritual as well. He believed it to be a magnificent idea.

It was clear to him that personally I had nothing to gain from his rising, which was beyond true. Whether he succeeded, or not, personally I wouldn't be affected.

The disturbing thing about that man was the complete lack of understanding of the most basic thing, the fact that every action has an opposite and equal reaction…he forgot about the simple fact of all spells, whether they are powerful, or not…they have consequences after their usage. But that's alright, it simply made my job easier.

Everything was almost ready for the ritual; the only detail that I had to take care of was a small one. The night before the ritual, I went to Echidno's chambers, which was fast asleep. He seemed happy, for after all, he was told that he'd help his father acquire greatness. They left, of course, the grim part of him dying in the process.

I whispered to him in his sleep: "My child, be warned, you are in grave danger. The ritual will either claim your life, or save it, should you be willing to slightly alter the circle at the point where you'll see the green tentacles. I am known as the Lady Dressed in September."

With that whisper, Antichoos's last thread of destiny was woven.

Chapter Eight
The Fall of the Mystics

The fateful day arrived. Most of the Mystics attended the ritual reluctantly, for after all, they distrusted their leader. Had they known his true intentions, they all would have run away…

They all gathered at the underground meeting place. The rest of the islanders didn't know much, only that the leader of the Mystics was planning to do something big, and they rejoiced because of that.

Antichoos, the greatest of them all, was already sitting on his throne, and I was right beside him. He had already drawn the magic circle for the ritual that very morning and because he was certain of himself, he didn't check the entirety of the circle; after all, no one knew the true purpose of the ritual, right?

The Mystics were all in place. Antichoos rose and cast the apocalyptic ritual spell. The entire underground chamber was showered with a red light as the circle was generated. Antichoos was overjoyed and laughed. He knew what he did, and was really happy about it…he really didn't care about his kin. The rest of the Mystics were frightened. Echidnos was determined. He did what he had to do, in order to survive, without knowing the consequences.

The red light turned green. One by one, they started to fall. Antichoos's last begging glance was to me, before falling down, lifeless. Echidnos was frightened. He saw his father fall down and immediately ran to his aid, only to fall onto the ground midway through, not knowing that everyone's life force around him, including half of the people of the island, were stored within him, which would one day lead him to be a frightening menace on this world.

To my great pleasure, I reigned victorious over the Mystics.

Chapter Nine
A Touch of Destiny

I, once again, lost consciousness and found myself in the pink space that was currently my home. But this time, I felt a little different than the last time I was here. I couldn't really distinguish what had changed within me, but I truly felt different. For the first time in a long while, I felt like I could indeed escape this coral prison. But for the first time ever since he appeared, no one else showed up, or left bread crumbs of any kind for me to follow… What am I to do next?

"What indeed?" suddenly a familiar voice resounded, startling me to no end.

"Are you…?" I mumbled, surprised.

"Oh, I see you remember me, huh?" he laughed.

"How could I forget you? Without your guidance, I'd never have made any progress…" I said humbly. Out of character, I know, but I deeply respected him.

"Glad to hear it, little darling! Now, for your predicament, you have made progress, indeed; you have conquered your fear, remembered your sister, who I will not utter her obnoxious name, and even had another audience with that has-been lord, the one who never gets bored sitting on that throne of his…however!" he paused.

I was in awe with him, once more. He was aware of all my ordeals, but unfortunately, he didn't sound impressed at all.

"That's not enough! You may have shown your growth when you defeated that loser, Antichoos, by using his own strength and weaknesses against him, that, however, will not be enough for the foes you'll encounter in the future. Your battle with the Mystics will seem obsolete, compared to the ones that are about to follow..." said he.

"Obsolete? For real? It was a pretty difficult battle for me!" I exclaimed loudly.

"Don't get me wrong, the only reason you managed to defeat him was because you played wonderfully well with his emotions and desires, but that's just it! You were in astral form and it was possible. When you escape, you'll be forced to battle your opponents directly! In time, warriors stronger than him will rise, warriors you might be forced to face, and that worries me, for if you are to ever repay me, you have to be alive to do so..." he concluded.

"I don't understand..." I said, completely lost.

"Right, of course, first things first! The reason no one appeared to guide you is that if you will and concentrate enough, you can actually escape this prison," said he simply.

"Really?!" I screamed happily, but after thinking about his earlier comments all of my joy was gone. "But you think it's too soon for me to leave this place, right?"

"That's correct, little darling, if you re-enter the world as you are now, you'll certainly perish..." he stated with the same calm voice as always.

"Then what do you believe is the best course for me to follow?" I asked.

"I like your choice of words, little darling!" he replied with a chuckle. "I believe that you should take advantage of your current predicament first, and then throw yourself into the real world, once again!"

"Take advantage of it? You mean to travel the world as an astral form?" I asked eagerly.

"Indeed!" he exclaimed, pleased by the fact I caught on quickly. "But you won't simply travel the world; you will shape it as you will, to prepare it for your grand entrance!"

"I see! I like the sound of that!" I said, pleased. "But how do I start?"

"Wonderful then! You can always start with a certain prince, whose name is the name of the colour of your prison, little darling!" said he cryptically.

"The name of the colour of my prison?" I repeated. "Coral, or maybe Corales?"

"Once again, you're right on, my little darling!" said he, quite impressed. "His name is Prince Corales, but that's all the information I can give you…the rest you must find on your own…"

"I like the sound of that!" I said. "After all, until my rise and downfall, I did everything on my own; that did not change!"

"Now, that's what I like to hear!" he agreed. "Make sure to tread lightly and trust no one, only yourself, little darling, and in due time, when you're ready, you can pull back the curtain for your grand entrance!"

"I can promise you that I'll do my best!" I said proudly. "Will we communicate again until that fateful day?"

"Next time we speak, it will be face to face, my sweet little darling, until then, know that I am rooting for you…ta-ta!" he said and just like that, I felt his presence disappear.

I was left alone again, but this time, my resolve was stronger than ever. I can do this.

Chapter Ten
Looking Back,
and Moving Forward

I had a lot of work to do. I felt ready. For starters, I had to find that prince, but that shouldn't be difficult. I'd become quite good at finding entities in my astral form. I couldn't calm down from my excitement. This time I'd make things right; I wouldn't move blindly, like last time. I will definitely meet him in person. I didn't even ask him as to why and how he ended up imprisoned...

I'll follow his instructions on how to become more powerful, but I won't stop there; in my astral form, I'll be able to manipulate people and all sorts of situations with ease.

But... Why is it? Why? I can't get him out of my mind... him, the one who imprisoned me... I don't remember his name, only his young, pretty face... Do I want revenge, or simply to thank him? After all, if that little one hadn't done what he did, I wouldn't have met him, and them; but most importantly, I might have ended up doing more harm to my precious forest, my loving home...

He may have sent me here, but thanks to him, I'm on my way to acquiring even more power. Thanks to him, I was able to venture to the very end of my fears and actually face them. Thanks to him, I was able to find my sister, even if it was only briefly. I bear no ill will towards him.

It's time. It's time to put my mind to it and get to work. The form of the Lady that's Dressed in September will once again enter the world. Beware.

I'll find you yet, my love, my life, my sister.